Raffi Songs to Read®

RISE AND SHINE

Words and music by Raffi, Bonnie Simpson, and Bert Simpson
Illustrated by Eugenie Fernandes

Crown Publishers, Inc., New York

Rise with the bluebird,

Shine like the sun.

Now's the time to
rise and shine.

Rise and shine,
The world's been turning
and everyone is waking.

Rise and shine,
On this new day
the morning light is breaking.

Rise with the rest of us,
Shine like a pearl,

Rise and show your love
all around the world.

Rise and shine,
Today is calling
and this is what it's saying:

Rise and shine,
Your friends are waking,

It's time for work
and playing.

Rise with the rest of us,
Shine like a pearl,

Rise and show your love
all around the world.

Rise with the bluebird,
Shine like the sun.
Now's the time to
rise and shine.

RISE AND SHINE

Words and music by
Raffi, Bonnie Simpson, and Bert Simpson

Moderately, with spirit

Rise with the blue-bird, Shine like the sun.___ Now's the time to rise and shine.

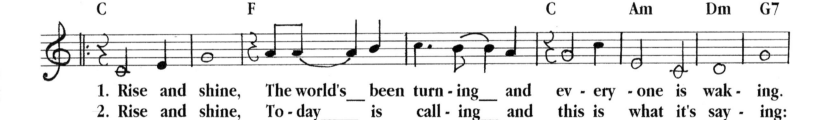

1. Rise and shine, The world's__ been turn-ing__ and ev-ery-one is wak-ing.
2. Rise and shine, To-day____ is call-ing__ and this is what it's say-ing:

1. Rise and shine, On this new day___ the morn-ing light is break-ing.
2. Rise and shine, Your friends are wak-ing,___ It's time for work and play-ing.

Rise with the rest___ of us, Shine like a pearl,___ Rise and show your love

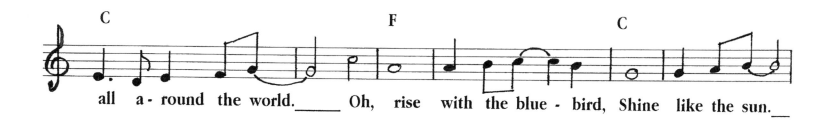

all a - round the world.____ Oh, rise with the blue - bird, Shine like the sun.__

Now's the time to rise and shine. Shine. Yes, now's the time to rise and shine.

*To our children, whose magic
lights up the day.*
— Raffi

*To Kim and Mike,
who rise and shine
For Robyn Mari*
— Eugenie Fernandes

Text copyright © 1982 by Homeland Publishing, a division of Troubadour Records Ltd.
Illustrations copyright © 1996 by Eugenie Fernandes
Front and back cover photographs © Colin Goldie, GM Studios

Published by Crown Publishers, Inc., a Random House company, 201 East 50th Street, New York, New York 10022.
Published in Canada by Random House of Canada Limited, Toronto.

CROWN is a trademark of Crown Publishers, Inc. RAFFI SONGS TO READ and SONGS TO READ
are registered trademarks of Troubadour Learning, a division of Troubadour Records Ltd.

Printed in the United States of America

Library of Congress Cataloging-in-Publication Data
Raffi.
Rise and shine / words and music by Raffi, Bonnie Simpson, and Bert Simpson ; illustrated by Eugenie Fernandes.
p. cm. — (Raffi songs to read)
Summary: An illustrated song celebrating the morning, the time to rise and shine and join the world.
1. Children's songs—Texts. [1. Morning—Songs and music. 2. Songs.]
I. Simpson, Bonnie. II. Simpson, Bert. III. Eugenie, ill. IV. Title. V. Series: Raffi.
Raffi songs to read.
PZ8.3.R124Ri 1996
782.42164'0268—dc20
[E]   96-29162

http://www.randomhouse.com/

ISBN 0-517-70939-2 (trade)
0-517-70940-6 (lib. bdg.)

10 9 8 7 6 5 4 3 2 1

First American Edition